taking a shot

a portland storm novella

catherine
gayle

night shift publishing

ISBN: 0990412679
ISBN-13: 978-0-9904126-7-0

dedication

For my Uncle John. I love you and I miss you, and I don't know what I would ever do without you telling me I have green hair.

1

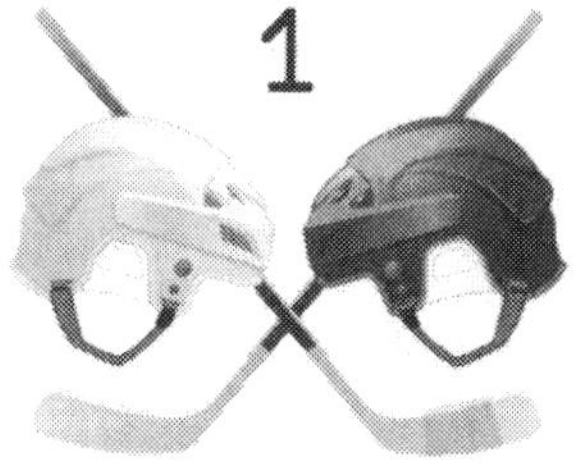

katie

THE TEAM STARTED to leave the ice after the morning skate, so this was my best chance, at least to just get it done and over with without Mom crying. I'd had enough of crying for a while—hers, my own, and everyone else's, too. Dad wouldn't cry over this—not in front of his teammates, at least—so I should be safe from tears for a bit as long as I could escape Mom's hovering and get to him.

Dad played pro hockey for the Portland Storm. Game-day skates weren't open to the general public, but Mom and I didn't count as part of the public around here. We were family.

Ever since I'd started chemotherapy treatments for my leukemia a few weeks ago, the Storm's general manager and coaching staff had been allowing me to come and watch the closed practices in addition to the off-day practices.

Mom always came with me. Sometimes it seemed as though she believed she could make me better just by being with me, which was ridiculous. Even these awful drugs might not make me better, so how could she? I wasn't exactly going to keel over and die while she wasn't looking, but she didn't like to let me out of her sight these days, as if she needed the physical reminder to know I was still alive. The only things I needed to remind me that I was alive were the aches and pains I'd been having.

I'd thought radiation was bad right up until the chemo started. Then I discovered that radiation was just the warm-up. Cancer treatments weren't for the faint of heart.

I figured the bigwigs with the Storm were just allowing me to tag along because I didn't have a whole lot to do these days. Maybe a little bit because they felt sorry for me, too, but this was one instance where I was more than willing to take advantage of some pity.

Plus, I thought it helped Dad not worry too much, and that could only help him to perform in games the way he needed to. Some days I thought my cancer was harder on my parents than it was on me. Not physically, so much, but emotionally. I didn't want to die, but I'd just kind of resigned myself to the fact that it might happen. They hadn't. Not yet, at least. And so they hovered. And worried. And cried.

I wished they would just accept that it might happen. That would be a whole lot easier for all of us.

With my treatments making me so sick, the school district had assigned me a laptop and had given me access to online coursework and a tutor who came to my house once a week for two hours. All I did other than my online classes and tutoring sessions was sleep, puke, try to imagine myself healthy again, and follow the Storm. Everything else had been put on hold—indefinitely.

That last bit, getting to follow the Storm, was the only part of my life keeping me sane, at least now in the early stages of chemo. I'd been going stir-crazy without school and Glee Club and all the other regular teenager things filling my days, and going to their practices and games gave me something to focus on other than how sometimes I wished it would just end, whatever that meant. They gave me something to believe in, and there hadn't been much of that lately.

My eyes followed my dad as he skated off the ice, gave me a brief wave, and headed down the tunnel with the rest of the guys. It was now or never. I didn't want to lie to Mom, but if I was going to go through with this, I didn't have much choice because of her hovering-to-keep-me-alive thing.

Cancer sucks and it kills a lot of people, and there was no question I might die, but it probably wasn't going to happen today. I was pretty sure I'd feel a lot worse than I did before it was all over. Not that I wanted to feel worse. I just wanted it to end.

I turned toward Mom and tried to look green, which wasn't all that hard these days. "I think I might be sick."

"Oh, Katie, today? You don't usually get sick so many days after a treatment…"

I put my hand up to my mouth, as though I was trying to hold back some puke. "Yeah. Today. I'll meet you by the parking garage when I'm done."

I didn't give her a chance to argue. I took off at a run, bolting up the stairs away from the Moda Center's ice with my hand over my mouth the entire way. I left my jacket, purse, and the throw blanket she'd brought with us to keep me warm behind with her. That way she'd have to gather it all up before she could follow. That should give me enough time to get to the bowels of the arena instead of making a beeline for the bathroom without her seeing where I was heading.

Sure enough, I got onto the elevator and the doors closed behind me without Mom appearing in the concourse.

I got off at ice level, and I made my way along the concrete walkway toward the Storm's offices and locker room. When I got to the double doors I was looking for, Daniel "Hammer" Hamm, one of the assistant coaches, was just making his way out and preparing to let the press in. They were standing just outside the doors, three men who'd become increasingly more familiar to me over the last few weeks.

I needed to get in before the press. They would be in there too long. I couldn't wait for them to finish and leave or else Mom would really freak out. If they beat me inside, I'd have to just go meet Mom and forget all about talking to Dad without having her around.

"Hammer!" I called out, still from some distance away. I was proud that I only sounded a little panicky, not like I was in a full-fledged freak-out.

He looked at me with his eyes squinting into a funny expression. I jogged the rest of the distance even though it left me winded so he wouldn't have to wait too long for an explanation, and so I wouldn't have to keep shouting. All three of the media guys spun their heads around to stare at me, too. I wished they would back off.

"Can I get in there for a minute?" I asked. "There's something I need my dad for. It should only take a few minutes."

He frowned. "What do you need that can't wait until he gets home, Katie? We have to let the media in…"

I reached into my pocket and showed him what I'd placed in there before leaving home this morning, keeping it hidden from the reporters who were craning their heads to see while trying to pretend that they weren't doing exactly that.

Hammer looked down at my hand and swallowed hard a couple of times. His Adam's apple bobbed in his throat, like Dad's did when he was trying not to get emotional. Then he nodded, and I put my hand back in my pocket.

"Let me go back in and make sure all the boys have clothes on so your dad doesn't have to kill anyone," he said. "Stay right here." He looked over to the press, who were waiting for their chance to go in and interview some of the players. "It's going to be a few more minutes, guys. Sorry."

A moment later, he opened one of the doors and let me in, closing it firmly behind me so no one else could follow. I made my way straight for my dad's stall.

He shook his head when he saw me, a slight frown turning down the corners of his lips. His eyes looked tired, with red streaks and bags under them. He'd only started looking like that and showing his age recently. I hated that I was the reason why.

"What's going on, Katie?" he asked.

I took a deep breath for courage. Then I emptied my pocket again and held the clump of my hair up for him to see. "It's starting to fall out. I don't want to wait and have it leave me with bald patches. I just want to shave it off." My voice kept cracking over the words, which sucked. I didn't want anyone to know how scared I was.

I'd woken up this morning and had nearly gotten sick when I found this big wad on my pillow. Heck of a way to wake up. Some more had come out when I'd brushed my hair, leaving a bald patch in the back that I'd had to hide with strategic barrette placement. I hadn't wanted Mom to see it. Or Luke and Dani, my younger brother and sister. They all worried so much, and this would only make the fears more real—bring them closer to coming true. As long as I had hair, we'd been able to pretend that I was just a little sick. This was going to shoot that idea out of the water, though.

It was unnaturally quiet in the locker room. The team had been playing well lately, winning more than losing, so that meant they were usually laughing and joking with each other when they were all together, keeping things loose. So I knew the guys were listening, even if their heads were turned away and they were pretending to keep busy with other things. It didn't matter if they heard, though. They could handle this—a lot better than Mom could, at any rate. Maybe better than I could.

Dad stared at the hair in my hand for a minute and then kissed my forehead. "Does your mom know you're down here?"

"No. I told her I felt sick and I'd meet her at the garage."

"She's going to kill me." His jaw was tight, like he was grinding his teeth, and his Adam's apple bobbed hard a couple of times.

I nodded. "It'll be better this way." Maybe not *better*, but at least easier.

"I know." He turned to Cam Johnson, one of his teammates, who was a few stalls down. "Jonny? You have your hair clippers here?" Jonny had kept his hair buzzed short, like a military cut, for as long as I'd known him.

"Yeah, gimme a sec." He reached overhead and took out a shoebox. He brought it over to us. "You want me to do it?"

"No, I'll do it," Dad said. His voice kept getting heavier, deeper. He was barely keeping it together. Maybe I shouldn't have asked him to do this with his teammates all around. Maybe I should have just kept trying to hide it with barrettes until I couldn't hide it any longer.

"Use one of the guards first until you get most of her hair off," Jonny said. "Then go back over it without a guard. That'll help keep it from pulling and hurting her." He winked and gave me a kind smile before he went back to doing whatever he'd been doing.

"Okay." Dad sorted through the guards in the box. He selected one and settled it over the cutting mechanism.

"Here, Katie," a deep voice said from behind me.

I turned to see Eric Zellinger, the team captain, holding a folding chair and a towel. "Sit down," Zee said. "We'll put this over your shoulders to catch the hair."

I nodded, biting down on my lip. A lot more of the guys were getting involved in this than I'd counted on. This was turning into something bigger than I'd expected, and it made me wish I'd thought it through better. All I'd been thinking about was Mom and her hovering.

He set the chair on the floor, and I dropped onto it. Dad put the towel around my shoulders. I removed the barrettes from my hair and stuck them in my pocket, not that I'd need them again anytime soon. I held the ends of the towel together in the front, staring down at my lap so he should have easy access. My hands were shaking, so I pressed my fingers tight to my chest so maybe the guys wouldn't notice how worked up I was.

The clippers buzzed to life by my ear, but then nothing happened. I lifted my head. At least half the team had stopped what they were doing to watch, some of them shifting uncomfortably. I didn't mean to make them uncomfortable. I just didn't know what else to do without upsetting Mom.

"You sure you're ready?" Dad asked. His voice cracked just like mine had.

I wasn't even close to ready and I couldn't make my body stop shuddering, but I said, "Yes. Do it." I tilted my head back so I could see him, and I gave him a big, fake smile before lowering my head again. I'd always been a good actress, but based on the way his eyes were shining, he hadn't bought it this time.

My attention shifted to Babs—Jamie Babcock, the youngest guy on the team, and the one I'd had the hugest crush on for forever. Or at least since I'd first met him when he'd started playing for the Storm. He looked as green as I'd tried to be in order to convince Mom I was sick. I didn't want him to see me bald—he might turn his back on me as fast as all my school friends had—but I couldn't kick him out. I was the intruder here, not him. Besides, I was going to be bald one way or another soon. Unless I was planning on hiding out in my bedroom for the next several months, chances were he was going to see me like that.

"Okay," Dad said finally, his usually steady voice shaking as hard as I was. He trailed his fingers through my hair in the back, as though he needed to touch it one more time in case it never came back.

I couldn't look away from Babs, and he didn't look away from me. He was sitting on the bench at his stall, his hands fisted at his sides, as the cool plastic guard touched down against my forehead. It glided back along my scalp, and large clumps of my hair rained down onto the towel over my shoulders. I caught a piece of it in my free hand. The long, brown strands still felt vibrant and alive.

Not like me. I hadn't felt vibrant in so long I almost didn't remember what it was like, and I didn't know if I wanted to be alive anymore if it had to hurt this bad.

I let the hair slip through my fingers and fall to my feet.

It didn't take long for Dad to finish the first pass with the guard, even with being careful around my ears. He powered the clippers off and removed the guard, tossing it back into the shoebox behind him. A moment later, the now-familiar buzzing sound filled the room again.

This time, I could feel the metal against my flesh. It was warm from the motor and a little scratchy, but it was oddly comforting. My scalp had been sensitive for days—a sure sign, according to my oncologist, that the hair loss would start soon. Dad went over some spots multiple times, then he rubbed my bald head to feel if he'd missed anything.

He turned the clippers off again, picked up a few strands of hair from the towel, shoved them in his pocket, and kissed the top of my head.

"You've got to tell me," I said. "Do I have any weird bumpy spots?" I needed some warning about things like that before I looked in a mirror. It was going to be enough of a shock to see myself without any hair. I'd always had a full head of long, thick brown hair, ever since I was really little. Even in my baby pictures I had a lot of hair. Mom said I'd come out that way.

"No weird bumpy spots," Dad said. He sounded gruff. I knew this wasn't easy for him. None of it was.

"Okay." I carefully took the towel off, looking down for the first time to see the mound of brown hair at my feet and surrounding the chair.

Jonny brought over a damp cloth and handed it to Dad. It was warm when he wiped it over my head, neck, and face to pick up any loose hairs.

I got up and kissed Dad on the cheek. "Is there a mirror around? I need to see."

Zee jerked his head to the side, toward another part of the room. "Over here."

I went to where he'd indicated and stared in shock at my reflection. It was still me—still my blue eyes, even though they seemed tired and sunken in, still my nose and my dry lips, still my slightly hollowed out cheekbones. But I looked like an alien. If my friends hadn't already dropped me, they definitely would now. Who would want to hang out with the weird alien girl? The lack of hair only seemed to emphasize the features that made it obvious I was sick. I let my hands run over my head as I turned to see myself from every angle.

No weird bumpy spots. Dad hadn't lied.

The clippers buzzed to life again, and I raced back into the main part of the locker room. My dad was in the chair. Jonny was shaving Dad's head.

"Oh, Daddy." I'd been able to get through losing my own hair without crying, but this time I couldn't hold my stupid tears back. "Mom really will kill you now."

He winked and reached for my hand. I held it, watching as his salt-and-pepper hair joined mine on the floor around the chair. Jonny finished shaving Dad's head a lot quicker than Dad had done mine.

"No weird bumpy spots?" Dad asked me.

I brushed away a tear and shook my head. "No weird bumpy spots."

He got up and left without saying another word, heading toward the mirror.

Jonny started to put the clippers away, but Babs got up and said, "Not yet. Do mine next."

"No!" I couldn't believe I'd just shouted at him, but I couldn't let Babs do that, even though the thought that he was willing to made my belly flip.

I loved his hair. It was this perfect blondish-brown shade, and he had it cut in a faux hawk lately that made me want to run my fingers through it. I couldn't do anything like that. Dad would kill Babs if he even looked at me funny, whether he'd done anything or not—not that he ever would. I was just another girl with a crush on him. He had more than enough of those to choose from. There was no reason he should choose me over any of the rest of them.

Babs was only a couple of years older than me—only twenty—but I didn't think age was really the issue for Dad when it came to the thought of me and a guy. He was stuck on the fact that I was still in high school, and he seemed to think I shouldn't even date until I was about sixty or seventy, or maybe not even then.

It didn't seem to matter to him that I'd already turned eighteen and was old enough that I could make my own choices. It happened two and a half weeks ago, actually, on the day that I'd started my first chemo treatment. Happy birthday to me. Here's some cake you can puke up later.

Babs stood in the middle of the locker room, his hands still balled into fists at his sides, staring at me. "I want to," he said. "I feel like it's the only thing I can do."

There wasn't anything *for* him to do. I shook my head, this time feeling like I might actually get sick. "Please, don't. I can handle losing my hair, but I don't think I can take it if you shave yours off. Plus, all of Portland would hate me."

He laughed, but it was an angry sort of laugh. Hurt. Like I'd hurt his feelings, which made no sense at all. He clenched his jaw, and it made his dimples come out. "Okay," he said finally. "But only because you asked me not to."

I took a couple of steps until I was standing right in front of him. "Thank you, Babs," I whispered.

"Jamie," he said. "Call me Jamie."

As he spoke, I could smell the sweet-and-spicy cinnamon scent on his breath from the mints he was always popping in his mouth. I was that close.

I stretched up on my toes and kissed him on the cheek, right where his dimple always showed up. "Jamie…thank you." I don't know what made me kiss him like that, but I couldn't seem to stop myself.

He brought his hand up, and I thought he might touch my cheek or my head. My pulse thundered like a wild stampede, and I couldn't breathe for wanting him to touch me in some small way, even though it was a crazy thought in the first place.

"You'd better back away from my little girl, dipshit," Dad said from right behind me.

Jamie dropped his hand to his side so fast you would have thought Dad had shot it.

I took a step back, almost bumping into my dad. "It's my fault. He didn't do anything." I turned to face him, and Jamie backed away to busy himself with something else. "Really, Dad."

"Your mother's waiting for you," he said, but I knew he was pissed. His eyes were more bloodshot than before, like he'd been crying. That was probably why he'd left for a minute—not so much to look at his own bald head.

I nodded. "Yeah. I'm going."

"Are you two coming to lunch with us today?"

"If I can get her to stop crying once she sees me like this. I'll text you to let you know." I raced out of the locker room before either of us started crying again and hurried past the reporters before they realized I didn't have any hair left.

2

jamie

MY CHEEK STILL tingled where Katie Weber had kissed it.

I tried to push that from my mind because her dad was glaring at me from across the table at Amani's Italian Restaurant like he wanted nothing more than to use his steak knife to cut off my balls and then feed them to me as my lunch instead of the chicken and pasta the waiters were serving us.

Amani's was our go-to restaurant for a pregame meal. It was a family-style place, where we ordered a few big dishes and all helped ourselves, and the staff always knew to expect us on the day of a home game. They made it feel homey—even if right now, Webs was doing his best to prevent me from feeling any sort of comfort.

Self-preservation seemed to be the wisest course of action after I'd almost fucked up and touched Katie. The last couple of months had really screwed with my head, with her being sick—mainly because there wasn't a damn thing I could do about it. That was the only excuse I could come up with for whatever idiocy had caused my lapse in judgment. Well, that and the fact that I'd completely lost all grip on reality when she'd kissed me.

Not that Webs would give a shit about my excuses. As soon as he had seen Katie take the seat directly across from me at the restaurant, he'd plopped himself down right next to her, and he hadn't stopped glaring at me since.

She had a scarf tied around her head now, a soft blue silky one that matched the color of her eyes. For some reason, without any hair on her head, her eyes stood out even more than usual. I didn't know if she'd chosen to put the scarf on or if her mom had insisted once she'd seen that all Katie's hair was gone. It didn't really matter, I supposed. But I liked how it made it easier to see her eyes. You could see a lot in Katie's eyes, if you knew to look.

Liam Kallen jabbed me in the ribs with his elbow to get my attention, and I snapped out of it long enough to take the bowl of pasta he was trying to pass to me. Kally was new to the team, and he was living with me now. He'd joined us at the trade deadline about a week ago along with Riley Jezek and Viktor Ellstrom. Kally and RJ had been playing for the Islanders, and Eller came over from Winnipeg.

Kally used to be one of the most prolific goal-scorers in the league—until his wife died. Everyone said that when she'd died, he'd stopped living, too. I wasn't so sure about that, but he was still trying to figure out how to score again, even though it had been more than a year since she'd been killed.

I put some of the pasta on my plate and passed the bowl on to my best friend on the team, Ray Chambers. Razor loaded his plate with about three times as much as I had and then reached for the salad in the middle of the table. I'd never met anyone who could put away as much food as he could, and that was saying something since I had six younger brothers and every single one of us played hockey and ate like a pig according to my mom.

Once I stopped staring at Katie and started eating, Webs finally focused more of his attention on his meal instead of inventing new and exciting ways to torture me.

Razor stuffed a massive forkful of pasta into his mouth. He had barely chewed and swallowed when he said, "So, Katie…you going to prom with the same guy as last year? It's coming up pretty soon, eh?"

Not only did Razor eat more than anyone I'd ever known, he was also quite possibly the most fucking clueless guy on the face of the planet when it came to tact. I kicked his shin hard under the table.

"Fuck, Babs!"

“Watch your fucking mouth in front of my daughter, asswipe,” Webs grumbled at him.

Razor shrugged his shoulders. “Sorry, Katie.” But he didn’t sound sorry.

I couldn’t make myself look anywhere but at Katie, though. She’d ducked her head down to stare at her plate and was as red-faced as she’d been while Webs had shaved her hair off a little bit ago. “I don’t think I’m going to prom this year,” she said quietly. She sounded sad. She always sounded sad lately.

Most of the guys started up their own conversations, turning their attention away from her. They probably didn’t want to embarrass her any more than Razor already had. But not all of them turned away. Zee was sitting on Katie’s other side, across from Kally. He handed her a basket of bread and asked, “Why aren’t you going?”

“Who would want to take the bald girl to prom?” She tried to laugh it off, but I could see the pain in her posture, just like I’d seen her fear through her bravery when she’d asked Webs to shave her head. She passed the bread to her father without taking any. “Besides, I’m not even going to classes right now. Out of sight, out of mind. They don’t even know I exist anymore.”

“I’m sure that’s not true.” Kally took a sip of his water and used his napkin to wipe his mouth. She gave him a dubious look, but he didn’t let it stop him. “You should go anyway. You could show them what they’re missing. Make yourself some good memories.”

Katie gave a tiny shake of her head. "I don't think I have that kind of courage."

"You have a hell of a lot more courage than you give yourself credit for," Kally replied. When she gave him a questioning look, he pointed at the scarf on her head.

She blushed. "That wasn't courage. That was fear of looking stupid with bald patches."

"Courage," Zee said slowly, but his eyes were on me and not on Katie while he talked, "is doing something you know you need to do even though you're scared to do it."

What was he getting at? I took another bite and stared down at my plate. That was better than looking at Webs with his ball-busting glares or at Zee and his meaningful glances that didn't really impart any meaning, at least.

"Yeah," she said. "Maybe." But then she started eating her meal and stopped talking, and that was the end of the conversation.

After we finished eating, everyone headed home. We had a game against Colorado tonight, and most guys take an afternoon nap on game days.

Kally had moved in with me when he'd been traded here because I had an extra room. I'd been living with Brenden Campbell—Soupy to the guys—but he'd moved across the hall to live with his fiancée, Rachel, and her two kids on trade deadline day.

It was nice having Kally around, even if he was closer in age to Webs than he was to me. He was a quiet guy, but he could cook, which was a definite bonus for me, and he didn't care if I had Razor over to play video games. Plus, he was a deep thinker. At first I'd thought he was a little weird, which wouldn't be too out of the ordinary considering he was Swedish. It felt like half the team consisted of Swedes these days, so I should know about how weird some of them could be. They tended to stick to themselves and not hang out with the rest of us, and I'd never met one who didn't have some crazy habit like sleeping naked with the windows open in January. But Kally usually had some pretty insightful things to say—the sort of things that would fuck with your head. At least he did on those rare occasions when he decided to open his mouth and say something.

Since the three of us—Soupy, Kally, and me—were all headed the same place, we'd driven in for the morning skate together in Soupy's SUV. When we were about halfway home, Kally turned around in his seat and looked at me with that intense stare he got when he was about to spout off something profound and life-altering and mind fucking.

"You could give her that good memory," he said. Okay, so maybe he really *was* weird.

I had always known everyone could see straight through me, and Zee and Soupy had been giving me shit about my crush on Katie for over a year, but Kally hadn't been around very long. How was it that he could already tell?

"Take her to her prom?" I shook my head. "Webs would kill me."

"This isn't about Webs. It's about Katie." Kally shifted even more in his seat, so much that he was practically in the back with me and had to be breaking the law sitting that way. "Hopefully she'll be fine in a few months or a year, and she can make a lot more good memories—but she might not be fine. She deserves to have this one, and her dad will see that eventually. He'll come around. But he can't give it to her—that kind of memory. You can."

"He's right," Soupy said, his eyes flicking up to the rearview mirror to meet mine. "And she needs a reason to fight. She looks like she's giving up."

I knew Kally was right, at least some part of me did, and what Soupy said about her giving up made me feel physically ill. But still… "How the hell am I supposed to get Webs to let me take her to her prom?"

Soupy turned into our parking garage. "You listen to what Zee said. You do what you know is right even though you're scared."

"You never know how long you'll have with her," Kally said. He turned around in his seat, facing forward again. "Don't put things off, because you might regret it someday."

AARON LUDWICZAK DIDN'T see the Colorado player cutting across the middle of the ice toward him, not even in the half-second before he got hit.

I didn't notice who ran him over. All I could focus on was how hard Luddy's head hit the ice when he dropped. The impact snapped his helmet off, and it went skidding across the ice in the opposite direction of his suddenly prone body.

"Fuck!" Scotty Thomas, our head coach, paced behind me on the bench while the trainers and medical staff headed out to check on Luddy.

The boys and I were all on our feet, trying to get a better look. After a minute, they had Luddy up on his knees and were helping him stand. That was a good sign—Luddy getting up—even if it wasn't completely on his own. That meant at least they weren't going to take him off on a stretcher. They'd had to do that with our starting goalie, Nicklas Ericsson, a few months back. Nicky had only returned from his concussion a couple of games ago. Not that you could tell anything about a concussion based on whether a stretcher was needed or not. And Luddy could still have one.

Hard to imagine that wasn't the case when you saw the way he hit the ice. The arena crew kept replaying the impact on the Jumbotron overhead, making sure we wouldn't be able to erase it from our memories.

The trainers brought him past the bench on the way to the tunnel, and he nodded at us. "Give 'em hell, boys."

Eddie Masters, the head trainer, stopped right in front of me. His eyes were focused on Scotty behind me. "We're taking him out of the game for concussion protocol. We'll know more later."

"Yeah. Right," Scotty said. "Fuck." He looked up and down the bench, and the two assistant coaches came over to him. "I don't want to screw with Zee's line. They've been working together too well lately."

Good. That was my line. Zee, Soupy, and I had made up the second line for big stretches of the last two seasons. I was pretty sure all three of us liked it that way, too.

"What about moving Kally up to take Luddy's place on the top line?" Hammer suggested. They'd had Kally skating on the third line this game, but he'd been all over the place while they tried to find a good fit for him, to find someone he could have chemistry with and get him scoring again…pretty much everywhere but the top line.

Scotty dragged a hand over his face. "He hasn't scored a fucking goal since he got here." He grabbed the clipboard from Hammer, scouring it with his eyes. You could almost see the way he was trying to piece together line combinations in his head.

"What better options do we have?" Hammer said. "At least for the rest of the game, and then we'll see what happens with Luddy. Besides, he and RJ are familiar with each other." RJ had taken over as the top-line center when they'd made the trade sending Sergei Ivanov and Pavel Spanov to the Islanders.

I didn't know if those two, Kally and RJ, had played together much when they were with the Islanders—at least not since Kally had stopped scoring—but they'd at least watched each other a lot for the last few years. That could help with knowing what the other guy would do.

"Yeah. Fine." Scotty didn't look too thrilled, but he didn't have much time to debate it right now—the ref was heading over to the bench to speed things along. "Kally, you'll be with RJ and Eller now. Jonny, you're moving up to Hank's line. Let's put this one away for Luddy."

He gave Zee a nod, and so he, Soupy, and I headed out for the next face-off. We were up two to one halfway through the third. Keeping this Colorado team limited to a single goal was a pretty rare feat. They tended to score early and often, which was a good thing for them since they had problems on the defensive side of things.

We really ought to have scored more against them to this point, though, considering how leaky their defense could be. The less time that remained on the clock, the more desperate they were getting to score. Our one-goal lead wasn't likely to hold up, but we needed to get the full two points for a regulation win tonight since we were tied with them in the playoff standings with less than a month remaining in the regular season.

The officials were set to drop the puck in our offensive zone, but Colorado had sent Matt Duchene and his line out to take the face-off. Duchene had owned Zee on the dot all night.

Zee motioned all of us over to him before we lined up, including Andrew Jensen and Keith Burns, our top two defensemen. "I have no chance of pulling it back. Not tonight. I'm going forward with it, straight for the net."

"Right," Soupy said. "So be ready for rebounds."

"Exactly."

We got into position, with me on Zee's right and Soupy on his left. If I could get past the Colorado *D*, I would be the first player to the crease. They should be expecting me to go to the middle and try to help Zee fish the puck out with all the difficulties he'd been having tonight.

Even though I knew Zee planned to shoot it on the net, he could have fooled me. The way he was holding his stick, it looked like he had every intention of winning possession the traditional way and letting our *D* set up our attack. I tried not to grin and give anything away, but everyone knew I didn't have a poker face.

I got lucky that the linesman didn't mess around with dropping the puck—I didn't have to try to keep a straight face for very long. Zee shot it forward just like he'd planned and confused the Colorado *D*. Soupy and I both got past our guys. I got to the side of the net just after their goaltender made a kick save. Too bad for him he kicked it out right onto the tape of my stick.

He was still sprawled on the ice from the save, so I roofed the puck. It went in just over the goalie's glove and under the crossbar.

"That was a fucking beauty," Soupy shouted at me over the dual roars of the crowd and the goal horn.

We all skated over to the bench and got fist bumps from the guys. Scotty gave us a nod so we stayed out for the next face-off.

Now Colorado was really pushing back. Their forwards were skilled, speedy, and determined even during their worst games, and tonight wasn't anything close to that. For the next several minutes, we were barely keeping our heads above water. If not for Nicky making one ridiculous save after another, they would have easily tied the game and moved ahead of us.

They hadn't, though, despite the fact that we were spending a hell of a lot more time in our own end than was good for us.

With only a couple of minutes left, RJ's line managed to clear the puck out of the zone so they could get off for a line change. Scotty shouted for my line to replace them. I was halfway on the ice when Colorado sent the puck careening back in. It hit Kally's skate. I had to hold myself dangling over the boards so we didn't get called for having too many men on the ice.

He shot it back to the other end and got onto the bench, and I was able to drop down to my skates finally.

They didn't waste any time retrieving the puck again and driving into our zone. As soon as they got set up, their goaltender headed for the bench so they could bring on an extra attacker. The way Colorado cycled the puck, it was like they were putting on a passing clinic. We couldn't quite catch up to them. Every time we'd prevent a pass one direction, they'd find a seam going the other way.

A hard pass to the point. I dropped to block the shot, and it hit off my shin and bounced right back to their *D*. The point-man sent it to the half-wall, then to the other defenseman streaking in for a back door opportunity. Nicky made the stop, but he couldn't control the rebound. Colorado retrieved it again and kept the pressure on.

We needed a whistle. Colorado kept cycling the puck, kept us chasing them for so long we were just trying to suck in air and not blow the game.

They sent the puck back to the other point. He passed it straight to the guy I was covering, who had his stick cocked for a one-timer. I squared up to block it, and this time it hit my skate. The puck sailed between both defenders and out of the zone.

They spun around to chase it, but I somehow found another gear despite my exhaustion. I beat them to it at center ice.

I took a swing.

The puck went in the net.

The Moda Center went berserk.

After that, with a three-goal lead, it was pretty much just a matter of running down the clock without giving them anything. My line headed back to the bench, and Hammer gave me a solid whack on the back of my helmet. "Nice work, Babs," he said. "Fucking right."

I was watching the action on the ice when Soupy elbowed me and pointed to a group of girls in the front row behind the penalty boxes. They were all wearing skimpy tops and looked so young I wondered why they didn't have dads like Webs running guys off. Each of them held a sign up to the glass.

Be my prom date, Jamie.

Tiegan + Jamie = 4Eva.

My Goal: Make a Storm with Jamie Babcock.

There were probably half a dozen more than that, too. I'd started ignoring the signs about a week into my rookie season; they were only a distraction. The boys never let me off the hook about it, though. Soupy and Zee kept trying to get me to auction myself off as a prom date for charity or some shit like that.

"Fuck off," I said to Soupy.

He laughed. "You could have your pick of them. I'm sure they'd all be thrilled to go to prom with you if you'd rather take one of them than Katie."

There wasn't a girl in the world I'd rather do anything with than Katie Weber, and he fucking knew it. Hell, apparently everyone knew it, judging by my earlier conversation with Kally. If they hadn't known it before this morning when she'd had her dad shave her hair off and I could barely hold it together, they all knew it now. I hadn't been able to look away, hadn't been able to hide anything I'd felt while watching it.

No poker face.

The horn sounded, marking the end of the game.

I couldn't get down the tunnel fast enough.

3

katie

MADDIE SHAW HAD latched on to me a few months ago when we first found out I was sick, and it didn't look like that was going to change now, even though I looked like an alien. Granted, she had always been a little different than most other little girls, or most people I knew, for that matter, so I didn't ever count on her reaction being what I should expect.

Maddie was Rachel Shaw's eight-year-old daughter. Rachel and Soupy were engaged and living together these days, plus Rachel worked for the Storm's GM, so I saw Maddie and her brother Tuck all the time—even more than usual now that I wasn't in school. They both had this bright red hair and a lot of freckles just like their mom, but that was where the similarities between the two kids ended.

Tuck was a few years younger than his sister, but he reminded me a lot more of myself, at least when I wasn't sick—full of energy, completely outgoing, and into everything and then some. As far as I could tell, the kid had never met a stranger, and he had a unique knack for getting everyone to like him.

Maddie was shy and quiet, though. She liked to stick to herself and read a book more than anything, or maybe talk with one or two people—but almost never kids her age. It was a lot more common for me to find her having a deep conversation with an adult than playing with another kid.

Maybe that was why she liked me—because even though I was technically still one of the kids in the Storm family, I was also one of the adults.

The last few weeks, I was gladder than ever that Maddie liked to hang out in a quiet corner. Chemo drained me, completely zapping all the life out of me. I didn't always have the energy to even talk much, especially late in the day when most of the Storm's games took place. By then, I was often talked out, and I could count on her to be off in a corner with a book and to welcome me in. But she always let be if I needed to just sit quietly.

That was what had happened tonight. When Mom and I had gotten up to the owner's box for the game, Maddie had been in her usual spot—in the opposite corner from all the other kids and their noise—with her nose buried in a book.

She'd smiled when I sat down next to her, seemingly oblivious to the fact that all my hair was gone and I had a stupid scarf covering my head to help keep it warm. "Want to share my blanket?" she'd asked.

I'd taken her up on the blanket. I was always cold these days, whether it was actually cold wherever I was or not.

That was exactly how we remained after the game, both of us cozy beneath the blanket, when I heard Jamie's voice behind me. I'd been expecting Dad and the other guys who had families watching the game up here to arrive sometime soon, but I hadn't been expecting Jamie. These days, he usually just headed straight for wherever the team was going for dinner along with the other single guys.

I couldn't stop myself. I whipped my head around to stare at him. He'd paused to talk to the kids near the entrance, especially Tuck, who thought Jamie was the best thing since Candy Crush. He had on a suit with a skinny tie like the Swedish players all preferred. Liam Kallen's fashion sense must be rubbing off on him now that they were living together. All the guys wore suits to and from their games—League dress code—but tonight Jamie hadn't taken the time to dry or style his hair like he usually did before leaving. It was wet and slicked back, which somehow only made him more perfect in my eyes. Thank God he hadn't shaved his hair off. I wouldn't have been able to see him like this if he had, and that would have been a travesty.

I had to get myself together.

Maddie put down her book and spun her head in the same direction. "Mr. Jamie had a good game tonight."

"Yeah, he did." I forced myself to turn around in my seat and look at Maddie instead of gawking at Jamie like a stupid teenager. He had more than enough teenaged girls staring at him all the time. He didn't need me to do it, too.

She was still looking over her shoulder at him, though. After a minute, she looked at me and grinned. "He's coming to talk to you. I have to go tell Mommy something." That was all the warning Maddie gave me. She got up from her seat, took her book, left me the blanket, and pranced away.

"Hi, Maddie. Bye, Maddie," Jamie said behind me.

My heartbeat stuttered.

What was he doing? After what had happened in the locker room this morning, he must have lost his mind to even think about coming near me. Dad was already emotional, and these days he was on high alert with everything concerning me. It wasn't like Jamie Babcock wanted anything more than just friendship, though—not that Dad would care about that. Still, it would be a lot better for Jamie to just stay away from me right now.

But he didn't.

Jamie moved between me and the chair in front of me, smiling in that way that brought out his dimples and made me tingle everywhere. "Hi, Katie. Mind if I sit with you for a minute?"

I checked over my shoulder. A few more of the guys had made it upstairs now, but Dad still wasn't among them. "I don't know if that's smart," I said. "My dad—"

"He won't be happy," Jamie interrupted. "I know. I'd still like to talk to you."

"Okay," I agreed, mainly because I couldn't tell him no. I wanted him to be next to me. I wanted to talk to him. I wanted to let myself imagine he could feel for me even half of what I felt for him. I wanted so many things that would lead to Dad killing him. Maybe it was selfish of me to give in so easily, but I didn't have it in me to stop myself right now. Who knew cancer made you selfish?

He sat down in the seat Maddie had just vacated. His arm brushed against mine, and I shivered.

"Are you cold?" He adjusted my blanket before I could answer, drawing it up close to my shoulders. His knuckles brushed against my chin, and he snapped his hand away like I'd scalded him. "Sorry," he mumbled.

I hated that he felt like he had to apologize for touching me, especially since he was just doing something nice. "It's all right," I said, unable to stop my smile. I was pretty sure I was blushing, too, and for a moment I wondered if my scalp would be all red like my cheeks when I blushed. "Dad didn't see."

"Yeah. Right." Jamie chuckled. He leaned over in his seat, resting his forearms on his thighs with his hands together. Then he sat up suddenly. "Listen, I've been thinking about what Kally said at lunch. About how you should go to your prom. He's right."

I shook my head, trying to keep my hot tears at bay. Enough with the stupid crying, already! I couldn't go to prom. Not with my bald, alien head—whether I wore a scarf to cover it or not. The kids at school weren't like Dad's teammates, and they weren't like Maddie Shaw. Teenagers could be unbelievably cruel. The second I walked in looking like this, I'd be mocked right back out the door, and I'd never live it down. I just wanted to hide away from them until I finished chemo and my hair grew back and I could pretend none of it had ever happened, and maybe even longer than that since they'd all forgotten I existed.

"Don't say no. Think about it."

"I am thinking about it. I'm thinking about how they'll all laugh. How they'll make fun of me because of my bald head. I'm thinking about how no one would want to go with me." As soon as they'd heard the word *cancer*, all my supposed friends had turned all weird. They'd dropped me like it was contagious or something, like they could catch leukemia from spending time with me. Mom kept saying that it was just that they didn't know how to be around me anymore, that they were scared and that teenagers just weren't equipped to handle some things that life throws at you. I didn't buy it. "I'm not going," I said emphatically.

"I wouldn't say *no one* would want to go with you."

The look Jamie was giving me stole my breath and made my stomach flutter, but not like it always seemed to do lately when I was going to be sick. This was night and day from that—all crazy electricity and jangling nerves, kind of exciting instead of gross and sick feeling.

"Don't tease me," I said. I scrunched myself up in my seat, trying to put a little distance between us.

I wasn't the only one who'd fallen head over heels for him pretty much the day he'd arrived in Portland. So had at least half the single girls here between the ages of ten and thirty.

He'd always been nice to me, but he was nice to everyone. If someone needed help, Jamie Babcock was the first person to notice it and do whatever was needed. Even when he'd been about to shave his head this morning, it was just because he was a nice guy.

I'd never really let myself believe anything would come from the friendship we had, even if I'd been daydreaming about him—and more than daydreaming—for two full hockey seasons now. "Don't make me wish for things that aren't ever going to happen. It'll ruin my image of you."

"I'm not teasing you. I want to take you to your prom." He reached out as though to take my hand, but I looked at him like he was crazy and he pulled his back. "They won't laugh if I'm with you."

It didn't sound like he was being arrogant. He was just stating a truth, and he was probably right. They wouldn't make fun of me. They'd be jealous, which would be yet another reason for them to talk about me behind my back.

I shook my head. "If you really want to take some girl to prom, I'm sure you won't have any problems finding a taker. You could have your pick of all those girls with the signs."

"I don't want to take *some girl* to prom. I don't want to take one of the girls with the signs. I don't want to auction myself off for charity to be some lovesick girl's prom date. I want to take you."

"But…why?" came out of my mouth before I could think better of it. Because I might very well be one of those lovesick girls he was talking about, even if I didn't bring signs to the games. And if he took me to my prom, you can bet it would feel to me like he was just doing it because he's a good guy.

"You're kidding, right?" He looked out at the arena where only workers remained, cleaning up the mess left behind by the crowd. He was blushing, which I'd always adored about him. Most guys his age wouldn't blush. But Jamie wasn't most guys. "You've got to be the only person on the planet who can't see straight through me if you really don't know the answer to that question."

He couldn't mean that he liked me. I mean, yeah, he had always been really nice to me and hung out with me at team events, but that was just who he was. He had latched on to Tuck and Maddie, too, once they'd moved in across the hall from him. The way he treated me couldn't mean anything…could it?

But why would he tease me about something like that?

My pulse was roaring through my head and these crazy, jittery tingles kept racing around in my chest and belly, and I couldn't force a single word past my lips without fear that

I'd make an absolute fool of myself. I could only stare at him and wish that he'd look at me again.

"Will you go with me?" he said finally. When he faced me, his blue eyes were so dark they were like the midnight sky, and he looked just as sick and anxious as he had when he'd watched Dad shaving my head. "Will you let me take you to your prom?"

"I…" My whole body shook so hard that even my lips trembled. I pressed them tightly together, trying to rein in my response.

That was when he touched my cheek with the back of his hand. I half gasped, half sighed and turned my head in toward his touch, seeking more like a greedy cat.

Of course, that was also the moment when my dad walked into the owner's box. Jamie's gaze lifted over me to the doorway, but he didn't take his hand away.

"I'm going to murder that dipshit," Dad said, but somehow his voice was growing distant, like he was moving farther away from us instead of coming closer.

Jamie's lips quirked up on one side. "Zee and Soupy hauled him out of here. Looks like they were waiting on him to come in like that. I don't know how much longer we have before he comes back to finish me off." He laughed. How could he laugh about something like that? "So will you? Let me take you?"

"But my dad…" No matter how tempting it was to forget reason and agree to go to prom with Jamie, I knew it was nothing more than a dream. There was no chance my father would ever agree to let one of his teammates take me out, whether it was to my prom or anything else. That would be an absolute nonstarter.

Jamie moved his hand, and his fingers dipped beneath the edge of my scarf. I wanted to pull away, but the look in his eye held me in place while he used nothing more than his fingertips to caress my newly bald scalp. "I'll deal with your dad. Let me worry about that."

Maybe having no hair made my skin more sensitive, or maybe it was the effects of the chemo—I couldn't be sure. All I knew was that my whole body was zinging with awareness from the way his fingertips were dancing over the skin an inch or two above my ear.

I'd dated a few boys before. I'd been kissed and touched in various ways, and it had all been exciting and wonderful and new, but this was so different. The way he was touching me was so much more intimate, and I felt more vulnerable and scared and raw than I could ever remember feeling in my life, but I didn't want it to end. Because it was perfect.

It made me wish I wasn't sick, that I was whole and alive and vibrant like I used to be.

I wasn't entirely sure what came over me because everything I'd said about not wanting to be the bald girl at prom was still a massive deterrent to going, and I had a very real fear that my father would do actual physical harm to Jamie, but I said, "Okay. Yes. I'll go with you."

He smiled, one of those amazing, shy smiles he had that made his dimples come to attention and left me wanting to kiss him. "Good. Now I'd better go deal with Webs before he hurts one of the boys."

I took his hand when he pulled it away from my head, holding it in mine for just a second. "Don't...don't let him hurt you, either."

"Don't worry about me," he said, squeezing my hand and sending a flood of warmth through to every nerve ending I had.

Before I could come up with a reasonable argument to convince him to leave by escaping through a back alley or some other means where he wouldn't have to go near my father, Jamie let go of my hand, winked at me, and was gone.

Mom came over almost instantly, like she'd been watching and waiting for Jamie to leave. "Do you want to tell me what that was about, or would you rather keep it to yourself?"

"Prom," I said.

That damn wetness popped back into her eyes, and she said, "Oh," all soft and touched and mom-like while she tried to blink the tears back.

"Don't let Dad hurt him," I begged. "Please."

Mom nodded and steeled her spine. "Not if I have anything to say about it." Just like that, her eyes were focused and she looked like Super Mom, ready to set the world right, at least for today.

I felt sorry for anyone who didn't have a mom like mine.

Heck, I felt sorry for anyone who didn't have a dad like mine, too.

They might drive me crazy sometimes, but it was only because they loved me.

4

jamie

"I ASKED KATIE to let me take her to her prom. That's all."

Webs hadn't stopped glaring at me since I found where Zee and Soupy had dragged him. For now, he was just sitting on a bench in the concourse. That meant he wasn't trying to close the distance between us so he could wring my neck or rip my head off my shoulders or any of the much more horrifying things involving certain parts of my anatomy I'd been imagining ever since Kally had put the idea of taking Katie to prom in my head this afternoon.

I didn't expect he would stay there very long. Not with the energy vibrating off him like it was. You could almost see it pinging through the air around him.

Zee was sitting next to him, and Soupy was standing off to the side—by all appearances, both of them ready to hold him back if needed. I didn't attempt to delude myself that they were doing it for my sake. It was for Katie, just like my somehow finding the balls to ask her and then coming here to talk to Webs about it was for Katie.

It was like Jim Sutter, our GM, was always saying: the Portland Storm wasn't just a team and a business. We were a family, and we took care of our own. It was my turn to do some of that *taking care of our own* bit.

"I don't give a fuck what you asked her," Webs growled at me. "She's my little girl, and you're going to stay the fuck away from her and keep your hands to yourself."

"No, he's not. Not this time, Dave."

I would know Laura Weber's voice anywhere. It was so much like Katie's, smooth and warm, but a little older and more careworn. I turned my head to see her marching straight for us, looking more determined than I'd seen her look about anything since Katie's diagnosis. She'd always been a force to be reckoned with, as long as I'd known her, but it was like she'd forgotten all of that when Katie had gotten sick. They'd all been losing a bit of their fight lately, the whole Weber family.

"She's still in high school," Webs shot back at her. "I'm not letting one of my fucking teammates, who's a grown-ass man, anywhere near my little girl."

"And she's got cancer." Laura didn't stop until she was standing between me and Webs, like she could somehow stop him from killing me just by standing between us. She planted her hands on her hips and stared at her husband while I tried to maneuver myself around her. There was no chance in hell I was going to let Katie's mom be a shield for me. She glanced at me but then returned her focus to her husband. "Cancer trumps your illogical need to keep her under lock and key until she's past her child-bearing years."

"The fact that she's sick is one more reason she's not going. She needs to stay home. She needs rest."

"All she does is rest!" Laura practically shouted at him. "She can rest the whole day leading up to prom so she's got the energy to go. But she's going. And Babs is taking her. And that's all there is to it because what she needs to do more than anything else is *live*—really live and not just survive like she's been doing the last few months."

It was almost as though she'd kicked me right in the nuts with that one. There was something in the way she'd said it, something that made it seem possible that if Katie didn't really start living again, then maybe she wouldn't survive it at all.

That's the thing with cancer, in my limited experience. It doesn't matter what the doctors say about your chances. If you give it the finger and keep going with your life, you have a hell of a better likelihood of kicking its ass than if you just give everything up and count on drugs and therapies and all that bullshit to fight it for you. At least it had always seemed that way to me, but I'd never had cancer before. I'd only watched my aunt go through it a few years ago—and I'd watched her lose. She'd shut herself off like Katie had once they'd started pumping the drugs into her, and it had eaten all the life out of her eyes until one day there'd been nothing left. She'd given up, and it had taken her away from my uncle and my cousins and my mom.

I couldn't handle seeing that happen to Katie. I wasn't ready to let her go.

It seemed like Laura's words had hit Webs just like they'd hit me. He looked as nauseated as I felt.

She moved a few steps closer to his bench and sat down next to him. "She has to remember that she's still alive. She has to remember what she's living for or we're going to lose her. This whole ordeal has just proven that, no matter how much we may want to, we can't protect her from life."

"I don't want to protect her from life," Webs grumbled. "I want to protect her from dipshits like him—"

"He's not going to hurt her, Dave, and you're seriously deluding yourself if you for one second believe otherwise."

I was a lot more afraid that I was going to be the one to get hurt in all of this—that I would end up with a broken heart. Someday, when Katie was healthy again and ready to get back to her life as it should be, she would move on. She'd probably head to LA or New York, somewhere she could pursue an acting or singing career. It was what she'd been dreaming of as long as I'd known her. I'd have to let her go, even though it would probably rip me to shreds. It would be worth it, though, getting hurt in the end. At least it would if it meant giving Katie something—anything—she could hold on to.

If it meant getting to hold her at least for one night.

"I don't like it," he said, looking straight through me.

"None of us likes it," Laura said. "It makes us feel helpless because we can't do anything. But for once, try to imagine what it's like for Katie."

I had to wait a long time for Webs to respond.

WE HAD SEVERAL games on the road after that, so I didn't get the chance to see or talk to Katie for over a week. I got to see Webs a whole lot more than I might have liked, since he was still more than happy to glare at me and tell me all the horrible and painful things he'd do to me if I did hurt her in any way.

I'd do anything to keep her from getting hurt, though.

Once we got back, I was really glad I'd taken Zee's advice last season and bought a tux. He'd told me there would be black-tie dinners, an annual Casino Night, and God only knew what else that I'd need one for during my pro career, and it just made more sense to have one of my own instead of wasting time trying to rent one. When you considered the fact that most hockey players needed custom-made pants anyway because we tend to have big thighs and asses, it really seemed stupid to rent.

Even still, I'd had to get some adjustments made to mine before Casino Night about a month ago. Everyone had warned me to get one with extra allowance for alterations because I probably wasn't finished growing. They'd been right. I'd added a couple more inches in height and about fifteen pounds of muscle since I got drafted the summer I was eighteen.

My tux still fit me now, though. My body hadn't changed too much since Casino Night. I adjusted the cummerbund and bow tie, looking myself over in the mirror. *Fuck*. I should have gotten a haircut, at least. It was a lot shaggier than it should be, and my faux hawk probably wasn't the best choice for an event like this, but there hadn't been time for that once we'd landed at PDX. I'd just had time to get home, eat something, and get dressed.

I rubbed some product between my hands and tried to get my hair to settle down—without much luck. Yeah, I really should've worked in time for a cut. If I was going almost anywhere else, I could toss a ball cap over it and pretend there wasn't a problem. Not tonight.

After a minute, I gave up trying to get it to lie flat or even to stop poking up in random ways. There wasn't much point.

I headed to the living room. Kally came out of the kitchen with a glass of water. He looked me over and nodded.

"You're doing a good thing," he said. "Katie's really lucky to have you."

He had it all wrong, though. I was lucky to have her. I tried to shrug off all the jumbles of things racing through me. At least for tonight, I had to keep it together.

"Got big plans for tonight?" I asked him. In the few weeks since Kally had arrived in Portland, there hadn't been too many times that he and I weren't doing something together on a night off. I'd been trying to help him get to know the area, to make sure he wasn't alone too much. It had to be tough, being the new guy on a team that had been together all season.

He shook his head. "Not really. I think I'm just going to drive around and see the city. I haven't had much opportunity for that."

"Yeah. Well, if you get bored, call Burnzie," I said. Keith Burns didn't believe in boredom. He always had something going on. Granted, probably not the sorts of things that would interest Kally, but still. I hated to see the guy alone, knowing what I did about how his wife died. It had been all over the news—the mainstream news, too, not just the hockey news. She'd had a flat tire on the highway and had been hit by an eighteen-wheeler while she was trying to change it.

He'd been gone with the team on a road trip. I hadn't ever talked to him about it. I didn't know how to bring it up, or if it would be stupid or rude of me to try to get him to talk. But everyone knew.

"I doubt I'll need to do that," Kally said, grinning.

I could never tell if his smiles were real or if he was just trying to pretend he was okay. How long does it take to get over something like that? I hoped I didn't have to learn anytime soon. "Yeah. You're probably right."

"Get out of here. Go get Katie, and don't worry about me." He swallowed a big swig of water. "I can look after myself."

I didn't have time to argue with him unless I wanted to be late picking up Katie. Considering all the threats Webs had issued lately, I didn't think that would be a good idea.

I pulled into their driveway about five minutes early.

Luke Weber—Katie's younger brother—opened the door. "You'd better come in and help or you'll never get out of here. Mom's fussing over her."

As soon as I stepped into the foyer, I could hear the commotion.

"This one looks so pretty with the color of the dress, though," Laura said.

"But it's *flannel*," Dani Weber—the youngest of the Weber siblings—said. You could almost hear a horrified shudder in her voice.

"Exactly. It's flannel," Laura countered. "Which will keep her head warm."

"I'm not wearing a flannel scarf with this dress."

"You could just stay home and not have to worry about what scarf to wear," Webs put in hopefully.

"She's going," Laura and Dani said at the same time.

"Not in a scarf that doesn't look right," Katie said. "I'd rather go with nothing on my head at all."

"But you'll get cold," Laura argued.

Luke glanced over at me, his eyebrows shooting up into his hairline almost comically. "See what I mean?"

He led me into the living room, where dozens of scarves of every color and fabric imaginable were draped over all the furniture. Laura must have started shopping for them the same day they got the diagnosis. Katie stood in the middle of the mess wearing an ice-blue dress that made her look like a princess. She even had on gloves, those long satiny ones that went up higher than her elbows. It was like she'd stepped right out of a fairy tale.

She looked up and saw me then. And she smiled.

My tongue got thick and dry. No one had caused that sort of reaction in me in a long time—no one but Katie. I cleared my throat. "You look beautiful."

She gave a tiny shake of her head, and she blushed. "Do you mind? If I don't wear a scarf tonight? I haven't found a wig I like yet, and I just…" Her eyes fell down to the flannel scarf in her hand.

"I don't mind whatever you do. You'll always be beautiful to me."

Webs shot me a go-to-hell look and grunted, and I was sure he was about to spout off another threat, but Laura's eyes turned soft and misty before he could. "But if you get cold…" she said.

"We'll take a scarf with us," I said, and I felt the weight of Katie's gaze fall on me. "And a sweater. Just in case." She had those gloves going up her arms, but her shoulders were bare. I didn't know how warm that dress was, but it didn't look anywhere close to as warm as my tux, and it was cool out tonight.

Katie nodded. "Just in case."

After a little more hemming and hawing, Laura finally relented and agreed to let us go as long as we took a warm scarf and sweater with us. I draped them both over my arm to carry them for Katie, and she picked up a small, white evening bag. I reached for her hand, but Webs cut between us and put a hand at the small of Katie's back.

He lifted a brow at me in challenge.

I turned tail and headed for the door. The sooner I could get her away from his prying eyes, the better. Part of me wondered if Webs had gotten them to install video cameras at the school gym so he could spy on us from home. I wouldn't put it past him.

"Wait!" Laura practically shouted behind us. "Pictures. I need to have pictures."

"They're already late enough," Webs said, but he turned around. "They'll have a photographer at the prom, won't they?"

"Have you *seen* the kinds of pictures those photographers take?" Laura countered.

"It'll be fine, Mom," Katie said. "You've got the pictures from last year anyway. And we'll make sure they take good ones. Won't we?" She looked at me when she asked that last bit.

I nodded. "Absolutely." Not that I had a clue how I could make sure of something like that, but I had seen Laura Weber staging photo shoots before at team events—

ordering people around like a drill sergeant. If I let her stop us now, we'd be here for another hour. Maybe longer.

She scowled, but she let us go.

When we got to my car, I opened the passenger door for Katie. Webs helped her in and shut the door before spinning around on me.

I had my free hand up in self-defense without thinking. "I swear I'm not going to—"

"Shut up, Babs," he interrupted.

I dropped my hand to my side, readjusting my grip on Katie's sweater and scarf. "Sorry."

"I just wanted to thank you. For this." Webs waved his hand haphazardly, encompassing everything around us. "And to say I'm sorry I've been an ass. I just don't know—" He cut himself off just as suddenly as he'd cut me off, and he blinked hard a couple of times. "I just needed someone to blame. Someone to take it out on. And I used you for that, even though it wasn't fair."

"You don't need to apologize." It might suck for me, but it made me really glad Katie had a dad who cared enough to be like that. That's how families are supposed to be.

"I do," Webs said. "And I really do appreciate what you're doing for my little girl, but if she isn't inside my house by midnight, all my previous threats are back in play."

I bit down on my tongue to keep myself from laughing. Moments like this, I was never sure if he was joking around with me or being serious. I figured it was somewhere in the middle. "Yes, sir. I'll have her back."

"You'd better. And if you fucking call me *sir* again…" Webs headed back toward the house without finishing his thought. "Take my little girl to her prom, Babs. Get out of here before I change my mind."

I headed around to the driver's side and got in with an uncontrollable smile on my face. I set her scarf and sweater down on the center console.

Katie put her hand on my forearm as I put the key in the ignition. "Was he horrible? Please tell me he wasn't awful to you."

I turned the key, and the engine purred. I might have been purring, too, because she was touching me. Shit, I was a mess. "He wasn't awful. He just loves you," I said finally. I almost said something crazy like *Just like I love you*, but I stopped myself. I didn't even know if I loved her. I knew I liked her a lot—more than I should, considering she was Webs's daughter. But tonight wasn't about me spilling my guts and making her feel like she needed to reciprocate. Tonight was about giving Katie a night where she could be a princess. "But we'd better not be late getting you home. I don't want him to turn my car into a pumpkin." Or me, for that matter.

5

katie

I'D NEVER IMAGINED I would think the school gym looked pretty, but that was exactly the right word to describe it.

The prom committee had strung tons of white Christmas lights from a disco ball in the center out to every corner of the enormous space, like a canopy of fairy lights hanging above us. Ribbons of red and white—our school colors—had been woven through them. They drifted down to flutter over our heads. The typical folding tables you'd expect to find had been covered with delicate tablecloths, and each of them had some sort of centerpiece—a flower arrangement, candles and mirrors, those sorts of things.

Even the chairs had been draped with cloth covers, so they fit the decorative scheme.

I held Jamie's hand tightly to steady myself and let my head fall back to take it all in as soon as we got inside. I wobbled slightly, dizzy from tilting my head back so far.

He gently tugged me closer to him, lending me more of his strength. "I've never seen a school gym decked out like this before," he said.

"Never? Not even at your own prom?"

"I didn't get to go to my prom." Jamie shrugged and flashed a dimpled grin in my direction. "We were playing in the Memorial Cup while it was going on."

"Oh, yeah."

I hadn't even thought about the fact that he probably would have missed out on his prom, among countless other things when he'd been in high school—things I took for granted. He'd played for the Windsor Spitfires in major junior hockey, so he hadn't even lived with his family for his last couple of years of school. He'd lived with a billet family.

My dad may be a professional athlete and so I had a lot of privileges that other kids hadn't, but for the most part, Mom and Dad had made sure our lives were as normal as possible. Even now, most people Jamie's age were off in college trying to figure out who they wanted to be when they grew up. He was already living it.

"Do you ever feel like you're missing out?" I asked. "Do you wish you'd done things a different way?"

"Sometimes." Jamie put his arm around my back, supporting me more than he could by just holding my hand.

I got goose bumps everywhere he touched me. It was like an electrical current was flowing to each point of contact, leaving me hyperaware. He met my gaze and held it so long I had to fight off a head-to-toe shiver.

"But then I remember," he said, "that I'm experiencing things most other people never will, so I should be grateful for what I have. And *then* I remember that if not for the path I chose, I wouldn't know you right now. I would hate that."

He made it sound like knowing me could make his decisions worthwhile. Like I really mattered to him. I hadn't felt like I mattered to anyone but my family in months. My heart thundered so loud he must've been able to hear it.

I bit my lower lip. "Should we go get pictures taken now, do you think? So we don't forget and my mom doesn't kill us?" I needed to redirect my thoughts—to do something so I could stop myself from wishing for more than what Jamie was really offering. Wishing for anything, really.

"If you want. I'll do anything you want me to do tonight, Katie."

He sounded so serious and earnest. There he went, being completely perfect again. It seemed like I was destined for a huge letdown at some point because I kept building his pedestal higher and higher in the sky, so high he would surely have to fall from it somewhere down the line.

But not right now. Right now, at least for tonight, he could be perfect.

"Then let's do that before I change my mind and don't want permanent reminders of how I look." Getting pictures taken as an alien princess might not be my brightest move ever.

The photographer was set up in the opposite corner from where we'd entered the gym. As we walked over to him, I felt stares following us each step of the way.

I couldn't make myself look at them. It would hurt too much to see their pity or disgust at my bald head, or their shock to see me at prom, or their jealousy that someone like Jamie would be here with someone who looked like I did right now. I didn't want to feel any of the emotions those things would call to the surface. Not tonight. So I stared straight ahead at our destination, not letting my eyes wander even the tiniest bit.

There were a few couples ahead of us in line when we arrived at the photo station. I watched the photographer work, but all the while I kept reveling in the corded muscles in Jamie's arm as he held me close to him. He made me feel safe and secure, just like my dad always had, but it was different, too. None of the boys I'd ever dated had made me feel that way—like he could fight off anything in the world that might hurt me.

They couldn't fight off everything, though—Jamie and Dad. They couldn't fight off leukemia. The drugs and doctors had to do that. And me. Somehow, I had to find the strength within me to fight back, and the courage, too, even though all I wanted to do was curl up in a ball and cry some days. Even though sometimes I just wanted it all to end. I had to figure out how to kick cancer's ass even though I didn't feel strong enough to kick a fly's ass right now. He was making me want to find that strength, though. I let myself lean on Jamie a little more than I had been, let him take a bit more of the burden of my weight.

Parker Jones and Sasha Marino were up first—the quarterback of the football team and one of the cheerleaders. The photographer and his assistant had them pose under a flower-lined arch, with Parker standing behind and just to the side of Sasha, putting his hands on her hips. It looked as completely forced and unnatural as it possibly could. I'd seen dozens of good pictures of those two over the years—they were completely photogenic—but something told me these would not be among their better shots. They definitely wouldn't be going on the keeper shelf. The photographer worked them through a series of three other poses, each as awful as the last, before they were done.

When Parker and Sasha walked past us, I realized I was still staring at them. Sasha caught my eye. She smiled, but her eyes kept moving back to the top of my head. I bit down on my tongue so I wouldn't say anything I might regret. I'd known before I'd ever agreed to come here that these were the types of reactions I would get. Expecting something and experiencing it were two very different things, though.

"Don't worry about it," Jamie said quietly in my ear once they were gone. "They'll get over it. If they don't move on, then they don't matter."

"I'm not worried about them."

"You are. You're all tense." He slid his hand up my back to my shoulder and kneaded, his hands touching my bare skin and making me shiver. "I don't want you to worry about anything tonight."

Right. No worrying. That was easy for him to say. Not so easy for me to do. I took a breath and tried to relax into him while we watched the photographer pose the next three couples in the exact same horrible poses he'd put Parker and Sasha in.

"I don't want to do those poses," I said to Jamie when the couple in front of us was finishing up. It was bad enough that I was going to be an alien in my prom pictures. I didn't want this guy's bad staging to make them even worse than they already would be.

"Okay. Then we won't do his poses."

A moment later, the photographer called us over and positioned us beneath the archway. Like everyone else, he kept staring at my head. I was starting to wish I'd given in and worn the scarf as Mom insisted, but more because I hated how they were staring at my head than because of being cold. He looked up at Jamie. "If you'll stand just behind her like—"

"We're going to do our own poses, actually," Jamie interrupted him.

"But, I..." He trailed off when Jamie turned me around to face him, wrapped both his arms around me, and enfolded me in a hug. "Right," the photographer said. "You're right, that's better. Just...here." He adjusted my arms so I was holding on to Jamie's rib cage and tilted my head so I was looking toward the camera, my cheek resting on Jamie's chest. "That's it. On three...two...one."

As the camera bulbs flashed, I felt Jamie's lips press down on the top of my head. My pulse came to a standstill and then jolted back to life. What was he doing? Why would he kiss me like that? No one had kissed me like that other than Daddy, right after he'd shaved my head—not in as long as I could remember.

"Beautiful. Stay right there," the photographer said. I forced myself not to snap my head back and question Jamie, and the bulbs lit up again. After a few shots, the photographer urged us to try something else.

Jamie tipped my chin up so I could look into his eyes. "Hold on around my neck."

I had to stretch up on my tiptoes to reach him that way. While I did that, my breathing going haywire, he dropped his head down so that our foreheads were touching and the end of his nose brushed the end of mine.

It was too perfectly sweet and intimate. I couldn't take it. The way he was looking at me, I felt like I was naked—not just my head, but all over—and he could see every part of me. Surely the camera must see it, too. I turned my eyes away, desperate to find a way to protect my heart from shattering like glass.

"No. No, look at him," the photographer said. "Just like you were a second ago. It was perfect."

It *was* perfect, which was why I couldn't keep doing it without falling apart.

"Just for a minute," Jamie said quietly.

I raised my gaze up to meet his again, mainly because he'd asked me to, but the sting of tears pressed at the backs of my eyes. He had a tear in his eye, too. The realization of that left me weak-kneed, and only Jamie's strong arms holding on to me kept me upright.

The photographer snapped a few shots, and then he asked for one more pose. I didn't want to do another pose. I wanted to walk away from there and not look back. Because even if the camera wasn't seeing the most hidden, private parts of me, I knew that Jamie was— parts that had been buried so deep that I wasn't even sure if I'd seen them before myself. The parts where all my fears had been hiding. The parts that weren't ready to die yet. The parts that still had some hope.

And that was terrifying. I didn't want to be so vulnerable. So exposed.

I tried to let him go because I needed to walk away and pull myself together again, but Jamie lifted me into his arms before I could. I sucked in a breath, my jaw hanging slack. I put one arm across his shoulders for balance, but I didn't need to. Jamie wouldn't drop me. He would never let me get hurt if he could help it—I could feel that in the gentleness of his touch and see it in the concern drawing his eyebrows together.

He sat on the gym floor, keeping me in his arms and positioning me on his lap.

"Yes, that's exactly what I want," the photographer said. He directed his assistant over to adjust my legs, wrapping them so that they curled around. She fidgeted with the way the skirt of my gown draped over them before giving a satisfied nod.

When she moved out of the shot, sniffling and brushing away tears of her own, Jamie said, "I want to kiss you."

I must have misheard him. My whole body trembled, and I shook my head. "What?"

His gaze traveled over my whole face—my eyes, my cheeks, my lips—as though he was memorizing every detail and etching them on to the surface of his mind. "Can I kiss you?"

"I—" I couldn't breathe for needing to let my tears loose, but I could never tell him no over something I'd been dreaming of for so long. "Yes," I whispered.

His lips pressed to mine, soft and tender, and the dam holding back my tears burst just as the camera's flash lit us up. He cupped my cheeks with both hands and used his thumbs to brush away the wetness on my cheeks. Gently, so very gently, he moved his lips over mine. I couldn't stop crying. I couldn't even slow the tears because I was too filled with emotions. They were of every variety, all filtering through me at such a rapid pace I couldn't even hope to keep up: joy, fear, hope, longing. My sobs kept coming, uncontainable and impossible to explain with words.

Our kiss tasted like cinnamon breath mints and the salt of my tears.

My eyes fluttered open when he broke away from me. His were so blue, so intense, so deep as he stared back at me, still caressing my cheeks with the pads of his thumbs.

"Do I need to apologize?" he asked, his voice cracking on the words.

My gut clenched at the thought of him apologizing for making me feel so incredibly safe and protected and loved. "No. Please don't."

Jamie nodded. He kissed me again, on the forehead this time, and I heard the shutter of the camera once more.

A boy whose face I recognized but whose name I couldn't remember stood over us, holding out a stack of tissues for me. I took them from him and wiped my eyes. "Thank you," I said, but my voice was all stuffy and watery.

He kept his hand out and reached for mine. "I can help you up, Katie."

When I was on my feet again, Jamie stood next to me and put his arm around my waist. He turned us, and in the area where the line waiting for the photographer had been, there was now a massive crowd—probably at least a hundred students, many of whom had been my good friends—all of them staring. Or I thought they had been my friends. Maybe they still were. Half of them were crying just as hard as I had been.

My breath caught, and I couldn't make my legs move. I leaned back into Jamie's chest.

"Are you all right?" he asked me, his voice soft and sure by my ear.

I nodded.

"I'm right here with you," he said, and he guided me toward this sea of faces I'd written out of my life.

Before I could process anything that had just happened, I got sucked into the sobbing whirlwind of people I'd thought had written me off as dead. Some reached for me to hold my hand as I passed. Others drew me in for a hug.

"We've missed you, Katie," they said.

They'd missed me? If they'd missed me, why hadn't they made any effort to see me? To support me when I might be dying? Why had they all been avoiding me like I had the plague? Maybe Mom had been right after all and they just didn't know how to deal. Maybe they were just as scared as I was.

A few kept saying, "You're so brave."

I didn't feel brave. I had felt terrified every single day since the doctor told me I had cancer, and my fear only seemed to grow by the minute. Even now, I wouldn't be here at all if not for Jamie—if not for him asking to bring me here, for him holding on to me and lending me his strength. I would be hiding out in my house and letting that fear take root in my mind. Letting it suck all the hope out of me until I wanted to give in.

It took nearly ten minutes for us to get through the throng and back into the main part of the gym, where they had the dance floor and tables and chairs.

Jamie must have sensed my exhaustion because he guided me to a chair and held it out for me. "Let's sit for a minute." He said it in a way that made it seem like he was just as tired as I was, but anyone with two eyes could see he was fine. He sat in the chair next to me and took my hand. "You are, you know. Brave," he added when I gave him a questioning look. "So brave."

He made me want to be brave.

6

jamie

I COULDN'T SEEM to take my eyes off Katie the whole night, not even when some of the guys from her school sat down and wanted advice on becoming a pro in their sports or when the girls came over and begged me to sign their arms or…well, some specific other places I had no intention of signing. The girls flirted and tried to get me to dance, but I was only here for Katie. I didn't want to be rude to them, but I really wasn't interested in anything they had to offer.

I didn't mind the requests for autographs so much. I'd gotten used to that by now. Everywhere I went someone wanted a piece of me. It was just the *other* pieces of me they wanted that got to me. It took some work on my part, but eventually, the overzealous girls backed off.

Every time one of the guys cut in for a dance with Katie, or one of the girls came to catch up with her, she seemed even more bewildered by the attention than she had when I'd kissed her. She'd been so sure that none of them cared about her anymore, when the truth was probably just that they didn't know how to tell her and show her. So often, cancer seems like a death sentence. How was someone our age supposed to react when we found out one of our own was in a battle like that? It just takes some time to adjust, I supposed. God knew I'd needed it.

I still wasn't sure what had come over me when we had gotten our pictures taken. I just knew that Katie had given a piece of herself in that moment, not only to me but to everyone who had been watching, and I hadn't been able to stop myself from kissing her. No—I could have stopped if she'd wanted me to. I just didn't want to stop, and she didn't ask. I wanted to hold her close and make her feel loved.

She'd laid herself bare in front of all of us, and the photographer had captured the moment. Katie had been crying a lot lately, but these were a different kind of tears. It wasn't just her fears and sadness keeping her locked up tight; it was so much more. Like everything under the moon that a person could feel had all crashed into her at once and it was too much for her to keep inside any longer.

I'd never witnessed anything more beautiful, so I could only imagine what the images would look like.

The thought had never crossed my mind that I might start to fall in love with her when I'd asked her to go to her prom with me. I had just wanted to see her come back to life. Well, she had, and now I was pretty much royally fucked. Getting Webs to let me take her to prom was one thing; getting him to let me really go out with her was something else entirely.

I was setting myself up for a huge heartbreak. I knew it. There just didn't seem to be any way to stop it from happening now. Maybe it was better not to try. Maybe I needed to feel that heartbreak so I could appreciate these moments—seeing her laughing and living—all the more.

The band finished their song, and the guy who'd most recently asked Katie to dance brought her over to me. Her smile was as bright as the twinkling lights overhead, but her cheeks were too flushed and her eyes were more sunken in than they had been only a short while ago. She was wearing out fast.

"Thanks, Shawn," she said, her voice winded, as she sat in the empty chair beside me.

He winked at her and nodded at me. "Any time, Katie." He gave an awkward wave and turned around, disappearing into the crowd.

I took her hand in mine. "Why don't we sit this one out?" I didn't want her to get so tired that she couldn't enjoy everything she wanted to experience tonight. She needed to pace herself.

She nodded. "That's probably best. I think they're about to announce the king and queen, anyway. Then they'll have their coronation dance. We should have a little while to get some rest in." Her eyes moved to the stage where a few of the teachers were gathering and taking over the use of the microphone from the band.

At least she wasn't going to try to convince me she wasn't tired.

I pushed a plate of fresh fruit in front of her and followed it with a glass of water. She dug in with no further prodding.

After a few bites, she said, "You should have some, too."

I shook my head. "I've already had plenty. I'm fine." Besides, as long as she was okay, I was okay.

A woman called for everyone's attention in the microphone. Once it got quiet, she turned it over to the senior-class president, a girl in a hot pink dress who I recognized as one of the first to talk to Katie tonight.

"As pretty much everyone should know, we had a last-minute revote on the prom king and queen." She took out an envelope and slid her finger under the flap, then pulled out a single card. "The results for both king and queen are unanimous on this revote. For the first time ever, we have no prom king."

A half-eaten strawberry fell from Katie's hand and back to the plate. She shook her head. "I don't understand," she said only loud enough for me to hear.

I thought I might understand, though, and if I was right it made me gladder than ever that I'd worked up the guts to ask her to come with me. But I just shrugged and shook my head, and I kept my attention focused on the stage.

"Now, as to the prom queen…"

The class president gave the band a nod, and they started playing again—the familiar strains of Bruno Mars's "Just the Way You Are." A few other students jumped up on the stage, and they all started dancing. I recognized a couple of them as members of Katie's Glee Club, and that was when I knew I was right.

Katie laughed, her eyes lighting up.

By the time the lead singer started singing, the crowd had parted and joined in the dancing, too.

"A flash mob?" Katie shouted at me in disbelief, her voice barely audible over the music. "Who are they mobbing? God, I would have loved to be part of this."

But she was about to be. She just hadn't accepted that someone could have done something like that for her…yet.

Sure enough, the lead dancers who'd joined the class president on stage jumped down to the dance floor as part of the routine, and the five of them danced their way through the path that had opened up in the crowd.

When the chorus kicked in, every single person in the gym—students and teachers alike—was singing along and pointing right at Katie. Her jaw dropped when she realized what they were doing. Fresh tears filled her eyes.

I put my hand on her back and leaned close. "Take it all in. Every moment of this."

After the second verse and chorus, the lead singer had joined everyone else on the dance floor. He took the microphone to the class president, and the band dropped their volume down and went into a holding pattern of sorts.

"We love you, Katie," the class president said over the music. "We all miss you, and we want you to know that we're all behind you—every single person here, students and teachers alike. You're not in this battle alone, and when you don't have the strength left, we're going to fight even harder. The Glee Club put this together for you with Mr. Jenkins's help, and we unanimously voted for you to be our prom queen." Then she handed the mic back to the singer.

Two of the dancers came over to collect Katie, but she was shaking so hard when she got to her feet that I worried she would fall. I got up with them, supporting her with an arm around her back. They led us out to the middle of the dance floor, and the crowd of dancers converged around us. Someone came forward with a wreath of flowers and put it on Katie's head right as the band kicked it into gear again.

Katie wobbled slightly, and I pulled her closer to my side, urging her to lean into me. She let most of her weight fall back, putting her hand over mine where I held her waist while they finished out the flash mob. As the strains of the music faded, everyone backed away until Katie and I were alone in the center of the gym. The lights dimmed except for a spotlight hitting the rotating disco ball above us and the Christmas lights draped everywhere. The band started into another song, a slower one this time.

"Can I have this dance?" I asked.

Swallowing hard, she nodded and sniffled, then turned to let me pull her close. "Did you know they were doing this?"

"No."

She rested her head on my shoulder. I rocked from side to side more than anything. I'd never been much of a dancer, and I didn't want to do anything to wear her out any more than she already was. She didn't seem to mind, though. She just held on to me.

I made note of every detail of this moment—the way the lights danced over her and illuminated her flowers and dress, the feel of her body pressed against mine, the soft flutters of her breath on my neck. It was all perfect.

At least for this one moment in time, she was my princess. No matter what happened, I would have this to hold on to.

katie

JAMIE HADN'T MINDED staying until the very last moment of prom, even though I was too tired to keep dancing. After our dance, when they'd named me prom queen, he'd sat with me at a table and let me enjoy everything the night had to offer.

But now everyone was leaving. Most people were going on to after-parties, but I definitely wasn't up for that. Plus, Dad wouldn't be happy if we stayed out too late. It was already eleven, so there wasn't a whole lot of time left before he'd be calling in a search party and hunting Jamie down. I didn't want anything like that to happen.

I was leaning on him a lot more than I ought to be as he guided me back out to his car. I couldn't seem to help myself. He kept drawing me closer anyway, so I knew he wasn't upset by it, and it felt really nice to have his arms around me.

We got to his car, and he opened the door for me. "Do you want to do anything else before I take you home?" He drove a flashy, black sports car. As far as I could tell, it was the one splurge he'd allowed himself after signing his first pro contract. Otherwise, he was still just a regular guy from Ontario, as completely ordinary and down-to-earth as anyone else you might meet.

But he wasn't ordinary. Ordinary guys wouldn't do all the things he'd done for me tonight. But then again, ordinary high school students wouldn't do the kinds of things my classmates had done for me tonight, either.

Maybe I needed to adjust my expectations a little.

I stifled a yawn while I tugged the skirt of my gown so it wouldn't get trapped in the car door. I didn't really want to go home yet, but I wasn't up to a whole lot right now—definitely nothing I could think of. "I don't know what else we can do at this time of night."

Jamie grinned, and both his dimples popped into place, making my heart pitter-patter. "We could go to Voodoo Doughnuts."

"Yeah?" I laughed and gave him and his tux a once over, then looked down at my gown. "Aren't we a little overdressed?"

Voodoo Doughnuts was one of the most iconic places in the city—a twenty-four hour doughnut shop that made the craziest doughnuts you could imagine and had a wedding chapel in their lobby.

"Does it really matter?" Jamie said. "We're in Portland."

He had a point. Years ago, the city, or at least the residents, had adopted the slogan of "Keep Portland Weird." They'd really taken it to heart in every way. "No, it doesn't matter," I said. "Let's go."

He closed my door and went around to the driver's side. I shivered when he opened his door and got in.

"You're cold? Here." He passed over my scarf and sweater. I still didn't really want to wear them, though; they would ruin the look of my gown. "Please?" he added when I hesitated.

I gave in without a fight, but mainly because I really *was* cold and it was almost impossible to warm up again if I let myself get too cold.

There was a wedding taking place in the chapel when we got there, so we actually looked like we belonged. Jamie led me to a small table by the window and helped me sit. "What's your pleasure?"

"The maple bacon bar," I said without hesitation. I had one years ago, and it was divine—an oblong, hole-less doughnut with a maple glaze and a strip of bacon on top—

but I usually avoided them because of all the fat and sugar. But if now wasn't a time to indulge, when was?

He winked and headed for the counter.

I got so caught up in watching the wedding taking place that his return startled me. He'd bought a whole box of doughnuts, not just one or two for each of us. The box was full, and each doughnut was a different kind.

"Is your blood sugar low or something?" I joked.

"Nah. I thought we could take some to your family, too."

Yeah, Jamie Babcock was getting to be more and more perfect by the moment. I melted a little bit at his thoughtfulness, particularly since I had a feeling Dad had been treating him miserably ever since the night he asked if he could bring me to prom.

Once I'd finished eating mine and the wedding ended, I really couldn't stop myself from yawning.

"All right, Cinderella," Jamie said. He stood up and collected the box, holding out his other hand for me. "Time to get you home."

I didn't want the night to end, but there was no chance I could come up with the energy to fight it. We headed out to his car and got in. He started the engine, but he didn't back out of his spot right away.

"Is something wrong?" I asked.

Jamie shook his head, but he was blushing. God, I loved how he blushed and got embarrassed about things. It helped me to remember that he wasn't that much older than me—not too far out of my reach. He took my hand.

"I just— I really want to kiss you again, without everyone watching and before I get you home. I don't think your dad will like it too much, and—"

"Jamie?" I had to cut him off because my heart felt like it would explode if he kept talking about kissing me instead of actually kissing me.

His eyes were so dark I couldn't tell the blue from the black when he faced me. "Yeah?"

I leaned toward him and tilted my head up. He angled his head at the same time, and we bumped noses.

"Sorry," he said.

"Knock it off and kiss me." I was laughing when our lips finally met, which was a thousand times better than crying.

He pulled away far too soon. Even though it had been just a sweet kiss, my pulse was galloping through my veins. He put the car into gear and backed out of his parking spot. "It's almost midnight," he explained.

"You'd better get me home, then." I didn't want to have to hold Dad back if we were late. I was too tired for that.

All the downstairs lights were still on when we pulled into the driveway. I knew better than to think Dad would have gone to bed without making sure I was home safe first. He liked to torture the boys I dated, both before and after our dates. No wonder I'd never had a boyfriend for long. My dad could be pretty intimidating.

Jamie held my hand the whole way inside, even as we went into the living room where Mom and Dad were waiting up on the couch. Both of their gazes immediately fell on us—Mom's happy, Dad's mad. Dani and Luke were both in there, too. Dani was reading a book and Luke was playing a video game on his Nintendo DS. They both looked up and then went back to what they were doing, but Dani had a huge grin on her face. Dad glared at our connected hands.

"We stopped at Voodoo Doughnuts before coming back," Jamie said. He set the box down on the closest table. "Thought you might like these for breakfast tomorrow."

Mom smiled at him. "Thanks. Did you have a good time?"

A good time didn't even come close to describing what tonight had been. I yawned as soon as I opened my mouth to answer her.

"I'll take that as a yes, then," Mom said.

Dad still wouldn't smile, though. "Practice in the morning, Babs. You'd better get home."

"Yeah. Headed that way," Jamie said. But he pulled me back into the entry hall with him before he left, drawing me in close to him like he'd held me when we danced. "Thank you for letting me take you out tonight."

Those stupid tears were pushing at the backs of my eyes again. I just wanted them to go away and stay away. "Thank you for taking me."

"When the pictures come in, can I have a set?"

I hadn't even known if I'd wanted a set of them—because of my alien head—but he'd insisted on buying the biggest package, not just the bare minimum for Mom. "You want them?"

"Yeah. Because that was the first time I got to see you—all of you. And it was beautiful."

"I—"

He kissed me on the forehead. Dad cleared his throat right behind me. Jamie and I both jumped.

"Good night, Babs," Dad said. He opened the door.

Jamie let me go and took a step back. "Good night, Katie."

He was through the doorway and Dad was closing the door behind him when I hurried to block him.

"Jamie?" I said.

He stopped and looked at me with a goofy grin, his blush and his dimples making him as adorable as ever.

"I'll keep a set for you."

He smiled all the way to his eyes. "I'll see you soon."

"Not too soon," Dad said gruffly. He closed and locked the door.

I stretched up on my toes and kissed him on the cheek. "I'll see him tomorrow at your practice." Before he could respond, I hurried up the stairs to my room and closed the door behind me.

Jamie had given me the most perfect night of my life, and I wasn't going to let anyone spoil it. Not even my dad. I didn't know how many more perfect nights I had left, but I did know this: I was done with forgetting about all the things I enjoyed and loved. I may have cancer, but that didn't mean I had to stop living. Jamie had given me that tonight. He'd given me a reason to kick cancer out of my life, or at least to give my all fighting for that.

I touched my fingertips to the spot on my forehead where he'd kissed me, leaning back against the door and sighing.

There was no way to know what life was going to throw at me next. Whatever it was, I was going to embrace it. Anything less was cheating myself.

Name	Position	Nickname	Number
Slava Lukashenko	Defense	Luka	2
Andrew Jensen	Defense	Jens	4
Peter Nylund	Defense	Ny	5
Ray Chambers	Defense	Razor	6
Keith Burns	Defense	Burnzie	7
Eric Zellinger	Center	Zee	9
Liam Kallen	Right Wing	Kally	10
Brenden Campbell	Left Wing	Soupy	11
Stéphane Montfort	Defense	Monty	12
David Weber	Left Wing	Webs	14
Jamie Babcock	Right Wing	Babs	19
Henrik Markusson	Center	Hank	21
Antoine Gagnon	Right Wing	Gags	22
Steve Matthews	Left Wing	Matty	24
Philippe Lafleur	Right Wing	Pepe	27
Cam Johnson	Left Wing	Jonny	28
Nicklas Ericsson	Goal	Nicky	30
Hunter Fielding	Goal	Hunter	31
Aaron Ludwiczak	Right Wing	Luddy	43
Cody Williams	Defense	Harry	46
Viktor Ellstrom	Left Wing	Eller	48
Jared Tucker	Center	JT	51
Kyle O'Roarke	Center	Chunk	62
Riley Jezek	Center	RJ	91

about the author

Catherine Gayle is a bestselling author of Regency-set historical romance and contemporary hockey romance with a New Adult feel. She's a transplanted Texan living in North Carolina with two extremely spoiled felines. In her spare time, she watches way too much hockey and reality TV, plans fun things to do for the Nephew Monster's next visit, and performs experiments in the kitchen which are rarely toxic.

If you enjoyed this book and want to know when more like it will be available, be sure to sign up for Catherine's mailing list. You can find out more on her website, her blog, at Red Door Reads, at Hockey Romance, at Facebook, on Twitter, and at Goodreads. If you want to see some of her cats' antics and possibly the occasional video update from Catherine, visit her YouTube account.

TAKING A SHOT, a novella, is book 2.5 in the *Portland Storm* series. If you enjoyed it, you can read the other books currently available in the series (listed in order), BREAKAWAY, ON THE FLY, LIGHT THE LAMP, and DELAY OF GAME.

books by catherine gayle

contemporary romance:

breakaway

on the fly

taking a shot

light the lamp

delay of game

double major

coming soon:

in the zone

historical romance:

twice a rake

saving grace

merely a miss

wallflower

pariah

seven minutes in devon

the devil to pay

a dance with the devil

an unintended journey

to enchant an icy earl

flight of fancy

rhyme and reason

thick as thieves

wanton wives

for a printable booklist, please visit www.catherinegayle.com

40621473R00050

Made in the USA
Charleston, SC
11 April 2015